Professo
Bounce

by Vivian French
Illustrated by Bill Ledger

Houghton Mifflin Harcourt.

Ben
(Sprint)

Ben is super fast! He can run five times around the school in less than ten seconds.

Mrs. Molten
(teacher)

Slink
(Combat Cat)

Professor Bounce

Professor Bounce is Mrs. Molten's friend. He has invented some impressive gadgets:

A bouncy bicycle—that can hop down the road.

A back-pic camera— that takes photos of things behind you.

A mechanical chef —that makes the best chocolate cake ever!

Professor Bounce had come to the school to show the children his new gadget.

"What is it?" Ben asked.

"It's my Food Copying Gadget!" said the professor.

"Let me show you."

The professor put a sandwich on the gadget.
"Are you ready?" he said.
"Yes!" shouted the children.

That looks tasty!

"I will just press this button," the professor said. A green beam surrounded the sandwich.

Then a second sandwich appeared next to it.

"Wow!" said Ben. "Can you do it again?"
Professor Bounce smiled and hit the button again.
At once, a third sandwich appeared.

I will just try one.

"Three sandwiches is plenty," Mrs. Molten said.
"Perhaps you should turn it off now."
"I am trying to," the professor said. "The button
is stuck!"

The gadget shook as extra sandwiches
kept appearing.
"It is very loud!" Ben shouted.
"I am getting a headache!"

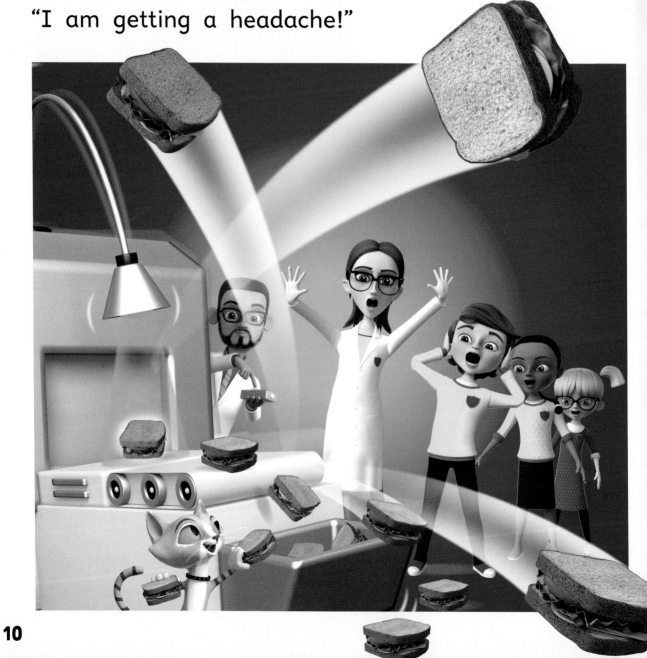

"Don't worry. We are not in danger," said the professor. "I just need to unstick this button."

The gadget began to whir and clunk.
"Hey, Slink!" Ben called. "I think you should move out of the way."

Professor Bounce dropped the controller.
The battery fell out and rolled away.

"We cannot stop the gadget without the battery!" the professor cried.
Mrs. Molten tried to grab the battery.
Ben started to chase it too.

"Phew!" said Ben. "I've got it."

Ben put the battery back into the controller.

He spun around to turn the gadget off.

Ben saw Slink by the gadget. Then he gasped.
There was a second Slink by the window and
a third Slink under the table.
There were *lots* of Slinks!

Ben turned the gadget off.

"What are we going to do?" Mrs. Molten asked the professor.

"I will fix the gadget," the professor replied.

"How can we help?" asked Ben.

"You need to round up all the Slinks,"
the professor replied.

The class began to chase all the Slinks.

The Slinks kept escaping.

"Ben!" Mrs. Molten shouted. "Use your super speed to round them up."

Ben ran in circles around the Slinks. He went so fast the Slinks could not escape.
Then he herded them over to the gadget.

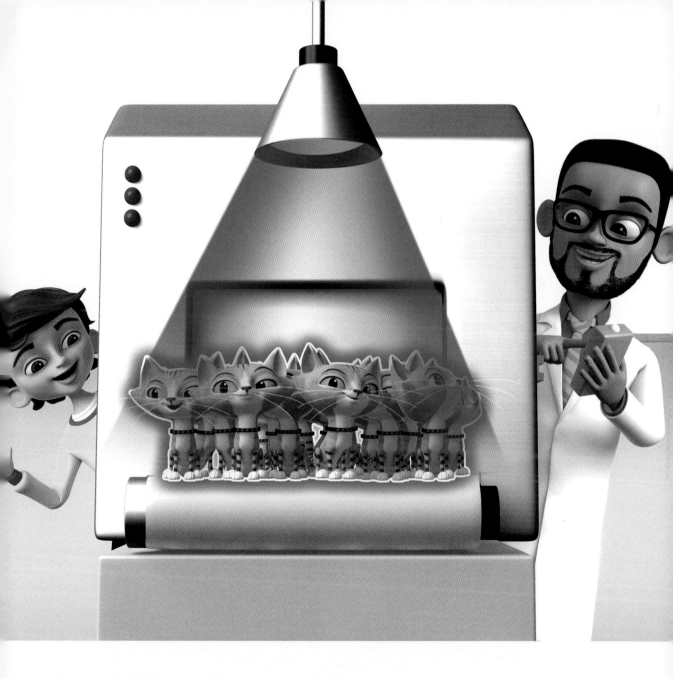

"NOW, Professor!" yelled Ben.

The professor gently pressed the button.

A blue beam surrounded all the Slinks.

Ben grinned. He could just see one Slink left. "Phew!" he said. "Everything is back to normal."

"How can we be sure this is the real Slink?"
Mrs. Molten asked.
Ben smiled. "I'm sure this is the real Slink.
He has eaten all the sandwiches!"

I feel sick!

Retell the story ....